ALLEY'S TREASURE HUNT

Love Others

Written by Laurie Zundel & Illustrated by Alice Kim

MW00902112

Thanks for choosing Alley's Treasure Hunt!

My Travel Friends® is designed to build character and educate children to inspire positive values worldwide.

Play and have fun in the exciting world of *My Travel Friends®* exploring through stories, videos, and apps. Learn reading, math, art, music, geography, physical health, and global cultures.

Search My Travel Friends® in the App Store for more great adventure stories, fun interactive learning apps, and audio! Teaching through music and technology.

GET THE AUDIOBOOK
on iTunes, Google Play & Amazon

Hear the characters come to life with Alley's Audiobook.

COMBINE PRINT + AUDIO
and increase comprehension by 40%

GET THE APPS
on iTunes & Google Play

MY TRAVEL FRIENDS
FUN ACTIVITIES FOR HOURS OF LEARNING

TO MY FIVE DAUGHTERS,

Kathy, the steadfast, compassionate encourager

Tamea, the dedicated, loyal giver

Jenean, the valiant, joyous light

Amy, the loving, creative visionary

Natalie, the kindhearted, courageous friend

You are my greatest treasure.
Love, Mom

WEBSITE www.mytravelfriends.com
AUTHOR WEBSITE: www.lauriezundel.com
TRADEMARK My Travel Friends #8632384
COPPA APPROVED

ISBN Paperback   978-1-939347-07-7

One sunny day, Slowpoke very slowly pushed a new adventure up the path. "Special delivery, snail mail is finally here," he said and handed Lettuce Learn a scroll. Excitedly, she unrolled it and read,

"You're invited on a TREASURE HUNT!
Real treasures are the best.
Look for treasures large and small.
The last will be the greatest of all!"

You're invited on a
Treasure Hunt!
Real treasures are the best
Look for treasures large and small
The last will be the greatest of all!

The treasure chest shook and rattled as she opened the lid, and a small Eiffel Tower popped up. The Captain found a note and read,

"The Eiffel Tower is CLUE #1. Now it's time to have some fun! Others are invited, too. Hurry and find the next clue."

"We're going to beautiful Paris on a Treasure Hunt!" Duke howled.

"And we're bound to have the best time ever!" Bonzo bounced and then paused with a puzzled look. "Ah, by the way, what is a treasure?"

Lettuce Learn laughed and then explained, "Treasures are special things we value, like the pearls my grandma gave me."

"And my fetching stick collection and, oh of course, my family. See, I even have your pictures with me," Duke howled.

"It's nice to be right up there with your fetching sticks," chuckled the Captain. "Buddy, land by that red box. I think it's our next clue."

They landed, and Duke raced to the box where he found a note. Suddenly, a white cat grabbed it from his paw and purred, "Purrr-fectly purrr-fect, I believe this is for me. I'm of royal blood and invited here by special invitation."

Duke stared intently and asked, "Haven't I seen you somewhere before?"

"I'm Alley, Alley the cat, a designer from London. I highly doubt we travel in the same circles, but you may have seen me featured in a New York fashion show," she bragged and swiped him with her claw.

"Ouch, it's all coming back to me now. You made me drop my juggling sticks in Central Park. Royal pain or not, I found it first, give it back!" Duke yelled chasing her round and round the box, "Now we're traveling in the same circle!"

During the wild chase, Alley dropped
the clue, and Bonzo picked it up and read,

"Inside is something shiny and new.
Dig down deep for Clue #2."

Instantly they leapt into the box, and tissue paper flew everywhere! "Look, all
you can see are the tips of their tails. I know you can beat that boastful brat.
Go Duke!" cheered Bonzo.

Lettuce Learn gave Bonzo a warning eye and said, "Be kind, and no name calling."

"We have to stop this dog and catfight," said the Captain.
Duke's head popped up as he proudly held up a toy sailboat and howled, "I found it!"

Inside is something
shiny and new.
Dig down deep for clue
number two.

Jumping from the box
with every strand of hair
standing on edge, Alley shrieked,
"Ouch, ouch, double ouch! The
static electricity is zapping me
and giving me a really bad hair day!"

Lettuce Learn said kindly, "Alley, let's be friends, and I'll help
you with your hair. Come join our team, and we'll find more
boats, just like that one."

"I'll think about it," she pouted and slowly followed behind.

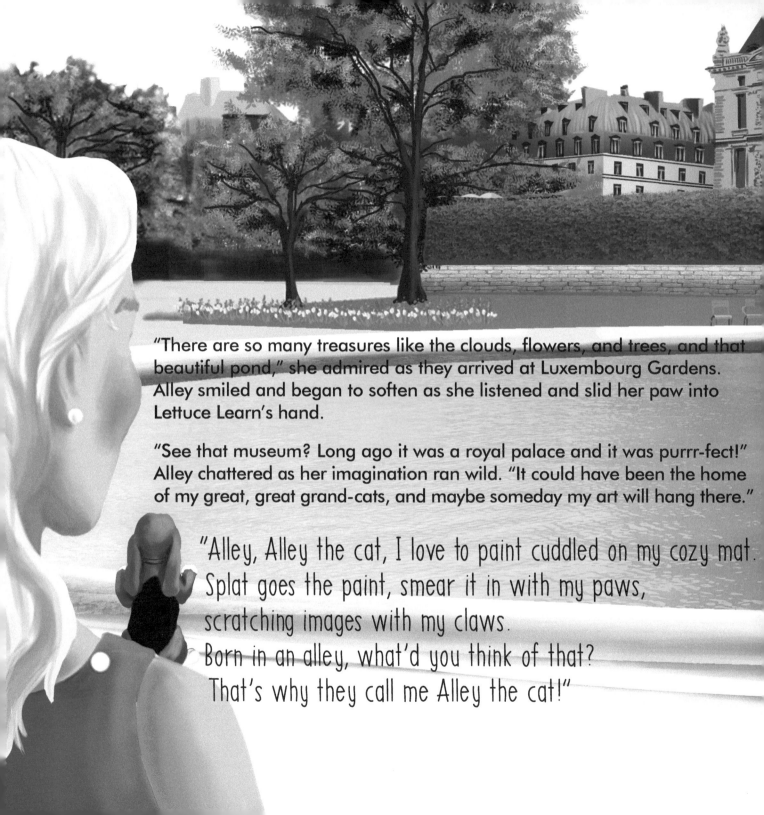

"There are so many treasures like the clouds, flowers, and trees, and that beautiful pond," she admired as they arrived at Luxembourg Gardens. Alley smiled and began to soften as she listened and slid her paw into Lettuce Learn's hand.

"See that museum? Long ago it was a royal palace and it was purrr-fect!" Alley chattered as her imagination ran wild. "It could have been the home of my great, great grand-cats, and maybe someday my art will hang there."

"Alley, Alley the cat, I love to paint cuddled on my cozy mat.
Splat goes the paint, smear it in with my paws,
scratching images with my claws.
Born in an alley, what'd you think of that?
That's why they call me Alley the cat!"

Hopping onto a toy boat, Bonzo flattened his body into a sail and caught the wind and circled the pond. Lettuce Learn squealed, "Bonzo's sailing around CLUE #3."

"Café Francais, my favorite bakery!"

Walking up the famous street, the Captain pointed and said, "This is the Arc de Triomphe, built by Napoleon to honor the soldiers who fought for France."

Duke admired, "Oh my, it's such a beautiful national treasure."

"The eternal flame is always burning to remember those who died for freedom," pointed Alley.

Bonzo whispered in awe, "They were brave, brave brothers."

"Yummy smells are making my sniffer go crazy!" Duke yowled as they entered the bakery.

"Bonjour Madame. May I please have a croissant?" Lettuce Learn asked.

"Why don't you try the special of the day," said the baker as she handed her a frosted pastry and read the clue.

"CLUE #4 is a painters perch, in Montmartre by the church."

Buddy flew them to the square as Alley squealed, "This place is purrr-fectly purrr-fect!"

"And beautifully beautiful," Bonzo bellowed.

Darting and sniffing everywhere, Duke howled, "All five senses are treasures for me. Hear, taste, touch, smell, and see!"

An artist called to them, "Mademoiselle, please, can you tell us the names of the artists and their paintings?" Everyone cheered as Lettuce Learn answered correctly, and the artist read the next clue.

"You earned CLUE #5. You're so smart.
Go to the place where you'll find this art."

"Now we're off to the Louvre," said the Captain.

Clue 5

While admiring the museum's beauty, a red Frisbee whizzed by. Duke's instincts kicked into action, and he jumped and caught it in midair. Flipping it over, he said, "Hey look, there's a clue taped inside."

"Find the Winged Victory without a head. CLUE #6 is there instead."

"Follow me," he howled as they walked into the sparkling glass entrance.

Clue 7

Alley climbed the Nike statue and popped her head on top as Duke howled, "You look like an angel."

"That's so nice of you, Duke. Maybe we should be friends, after all." Alley hopped down and smiled.

"Trying to be more like an angel is good for both of us," he howled and read,

"Find CLUE #7, a lady with style.
Her famous face has a priceless smile."

Bonzo bellowed, "I believe it is the Mona Lisa."

The Captain led them to a special room and pointed, "You are now looking at one of the most famous art treasures in the world."

Clue 8

"She may have the most famous smile, but yours is much prettier," Duke whispered in Lettuce Learn's ear. Then a museum guard handed them a map as he read the next clue.

"You just found CLUE #8. Follow this map and don't be late."

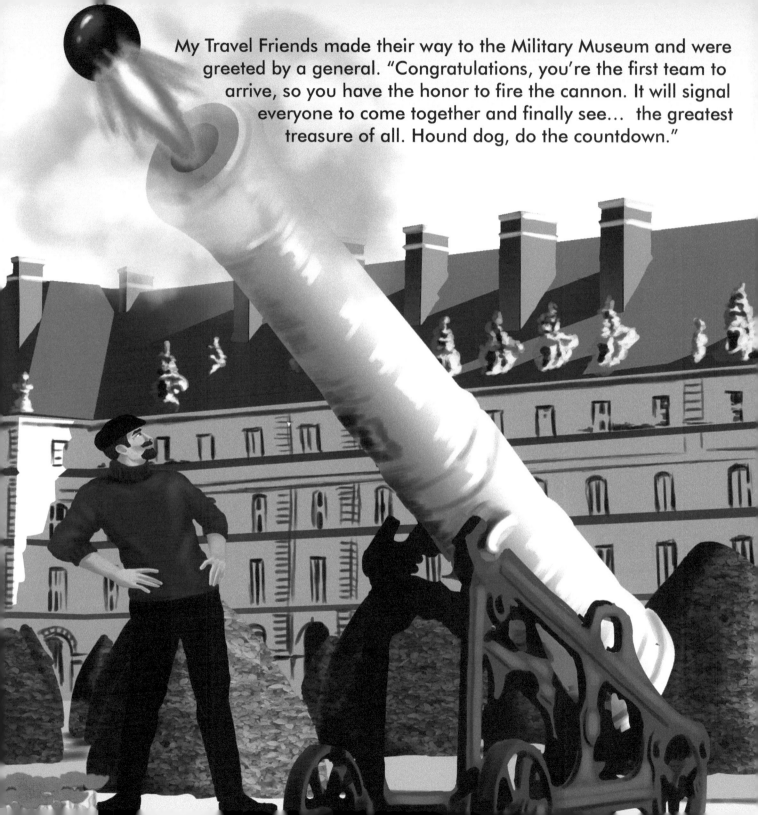

My Travel Friends made their way to the Military Museum and were greeted by a general. "Congratulations, you're the first team to arrive, so you have the honor to fire the cannon. It will signal everyone to come together and finally see... the greatest treasure of all. Hound dog, do the countdown."

"10, 9, 8, 7, 6, 5, 4, 3, 2, 1 BLASTOFF!" howled Duke as everyone cheered and the cannon ball flew across the sky.

The map led them inside as Alley pointed and joked, "Look, here comes a knight in shining armor!"

"Fair damsels, come quickly and try on these hats," said the knight.

Alley squealed, "I love hats, and these are the oldest I've ever seen. I'll try this one."

"There are only two clues left, and the race is so very close. Other teams are now arriving, so to keep your lead, you must stay sharp and be smart," he said as Lettuce Learn put on the knight's helmet and a bell dropped to the ground.

"This clue has a nice ring to it," Duke laughed and then read. "Listen to the bells chime. At Notre Dame is CLUE #9."

"Rush hour traffic is getting heavy, so let's take the Seine," said the Captain.

Buddy transformed into a boat and whisked them downstream as Bonzo blurted, "We're on a breezy boat, bouncing over blue waves and under beautiful bridges."

Suddenly, a gust of wind blew Alley's hat into the water, and without thinking she jumped in after it. SPLAT! She hit the water with a belly flop and yelled, "Ouch, ouch, ouch, triple ouch! Oh please help me, I can't swim."

SPLASH! Duke jumped in and paddled toward her, yowling, "Dog paddle and keep your head above water!"

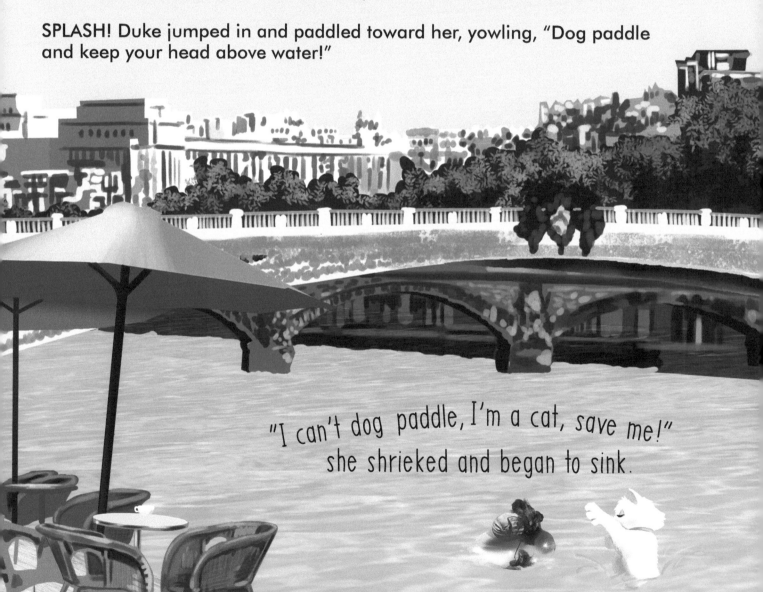

"I can't dog paddle, I'm a cat, save me!"
she shrieked and began to sink.

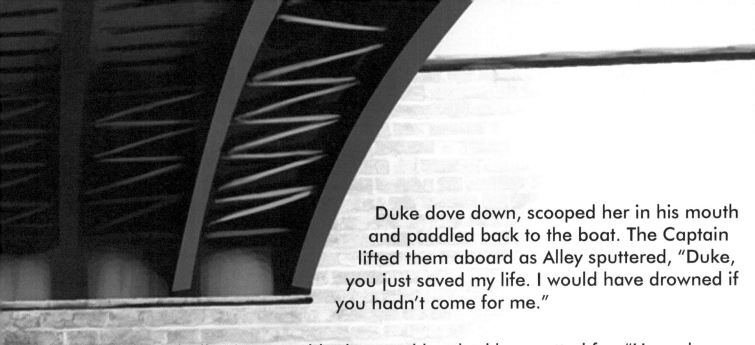

Duke dove down, scooped her in his mouth and paddled back to the boat. The Captain lifted them aboard as Alley sputtered, "Duke, you just saved my life. I would have drowned if you hadn't come for me."

Then, they wrapped Alley in warm blankets and brushed her matted fur. "Hey, where did all your fluff go? You look like a drowned rat to me," Bonzo blurted. "Oh, you're having a really bad hair day."

"Blunt Bonzo, if you weren't just such a baby frog, I'd bat you one," she shivered and then gave him a smile. "I may look like a drowned rat but really, I'm just a grateful cat. And as for all my fluff, it sailed down the river with my pride."

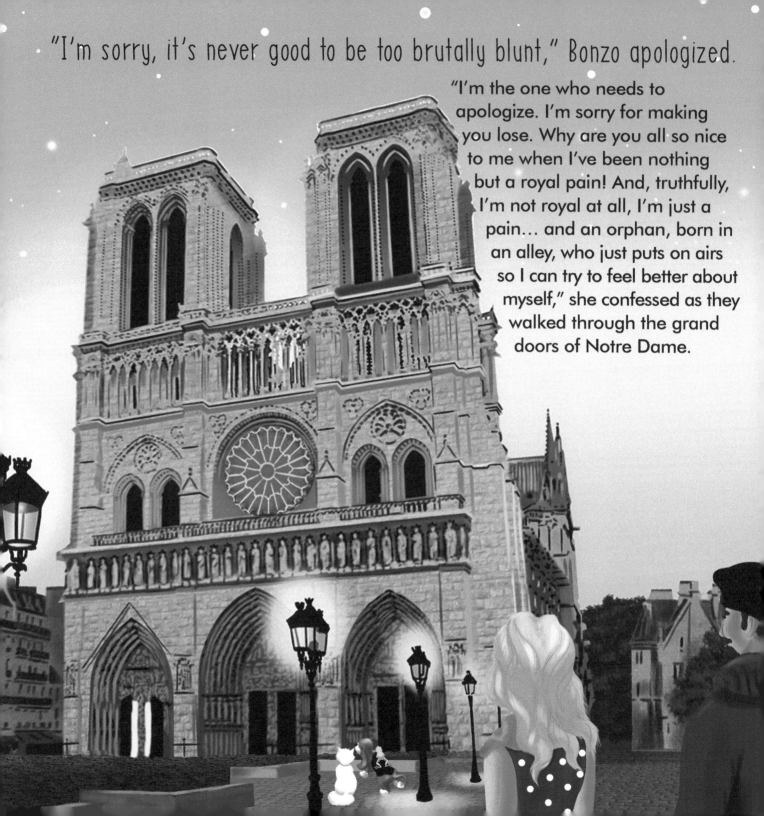

"I'm sorry, it's never good to be too brutally blunt," Bonzo apologized. "I'm the one who needs to apologize. I'm sorry for making you lose. Why are you all so nice to me when I've been nothing but a royal pain! And, truthfully, I'm not royal at all, I'm just a pain... and an orphan, born in an alley, who just puts on airs so I can try to feel better about myself," she confessed as they walked through the grand doors of Notre Dame.

Glistening colors of light streamed through the rosebud window as the sun began to set. "Alley, to answer your question, we're choosing to love you because LOVE helps heal the world. It's the greatest gift we can ever share, give, or receive," Lettuce Learn whispered as the last clue floated down like a feather from the dome ceiling.

Alley caught it in the air and read, "Clue #10, you'll see the light at the Eiffel Tower tonight!"

Clue 10, you'll see the light at the Eiffel Tower tonight

Large crowds and all the teams cheered as the tower began playing music and flashing colors. "We're on time. Hey Alley, we're right back where we started. We've come full circle," Duke joked, howling with laughter.

Alley giggled and joked back, "If you don't mind, this is the purrr-fectly purrr-fect time for me to start chasing my dreams

and traveling in a new circle with My Travel Friends."

Fireworks exploded as Alley read the message bursting across the sky, "Of all life's treasures large and small

LOVE IS THE GREATEST TREASURE OF ALL!"

"Alley, Alley the cat,
I love everything from this to that.
Love, love, love brings joy to faces,
love brings life in everyday places.
I love you, what do you think of that,
love heals the world and that's a fact!"

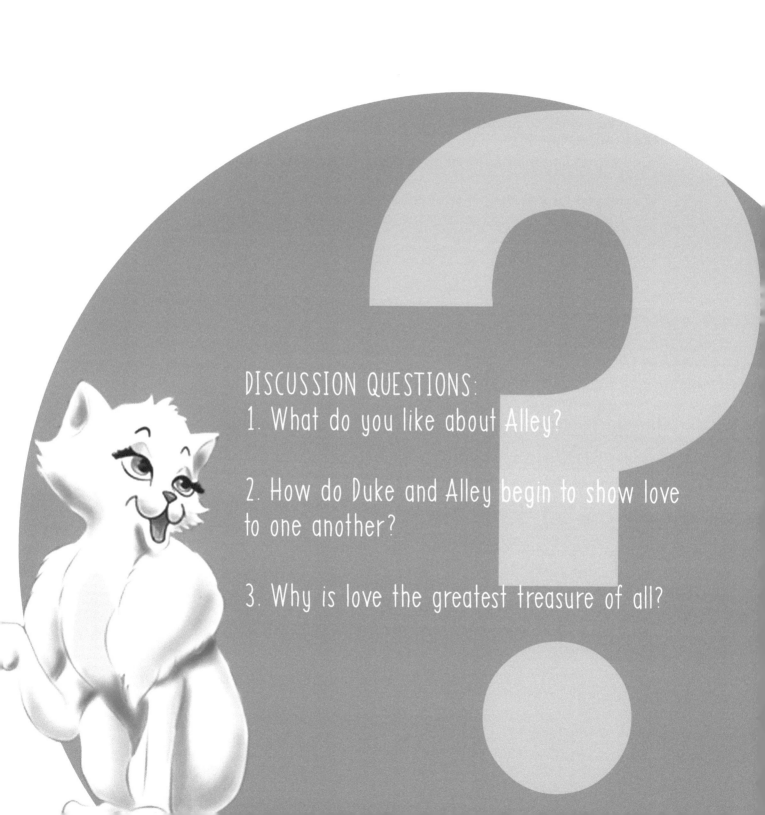

DISCUSSION QUESTIONS:
1. What do you like about Alley?

2. How do Duke and Alley begin to show love to one another?

3. Why is love the greatest treasure of all?

DEAR PARENTS

I am so excited to inspire your child's imagination through My Travel Friends. My hope is to partner with you in building your child's character and expanding their knowledge and appreciation of our world.

Thank you for investing in your child, our future.

Laurie

Laurie Zundel is an innovative educator and author. Her lifelong passion is to make learning fun and encourage children to discover their unique gifts and strengths, nurturing growth and self-esteem. Nothing brings her greater joy than seeing the face of a child light up with new learning and discovery.

My Travel Friends merges her passion and love for life, children, travel, music, writing, and artistic education. Laurie uses different learning styles to build character and spread positive values. Her imaginative visuals make learning fun, and her original music makes it stick!

Laurie and her husband Larry live in Seattle and enjoy life with their growing family of 5 daughters and 15 grandchildren.

www.lauriezundel.com